∞

CHEAP CHILLS
BOOK TWO

∞

BY
K. N. BUCK

Airleaf
Publishing

airleaf.com

In Memory of Mr. and Mrs. Wayne E. Buck,
My Father & Mother.
Thank You

Also By K. N. Buck

CHEAP CHILLS THRILLER SERIES:

HOUSE OF MIRRORS (ISBN 1-59453-901-4)

Available through your local book retailer or online at:
www.airleaf. com

Just like a glass of cloudy water,
When left unstirred
Becomes clear,
So is the mind,
When left undisturbed, will
Find its own clearness.

K. N. BUCK

K. N. BUCK

BOOK TWO

THE GATEKEEPER

A Cheap Chills Thriller

HOSTED BY

PROF. T. LEEZARD

TABLE OF CONTENTS

* INTRO *

"Right this way, right this way, have your tickets ready. Watch your step and move along. No crowding please. The show will begin shortly.

My name is Proffessor T. LeeZard and I'm here to gurantee that what you are about to hear is true. I am about to take you on a journey to a strange place and time, where anything is possible.

Step right up. Don't be shy. I see some new faces in the crowd, along with those that dare to return for more. Faces that have seen the unbelievable and those that are about to. Form one line please, the show is about to begin.

Right this way, right this way. There's room down front for a few more. Now, if everyone is settled and comfortable, let the unsettling begin. As always, with a wave of THE DRAGONSTICK cane, my trusted aid, may

I present to you, the story of two brothers and their race toward death with **THE GATEKEEPER.**"

Proffessor T. LeeZard

"The journey home to Favisham."

* CHAPTER ONE *

The black passenger coach rolled on at a steady speed, with the sound of horses making their way through the mud and rain. A steady stream of white breath steamed from each of the horses panting nostrils. The driver, a small chubby little man wearing a long black cloak, sat on top of the carriage. With one hand on the reins and the other holding a whip, he continually tried to coax more speed from the team of exhausted horses. The driver would use the whip on the backside of his lead horse and that would control the rest of the team.

It was mid winter, but an early thaw had melted most of the ice and snow. The pounding rain that had drenched this region for the last three days had finally turned to light drizzle. The driver struggled to keep the wooden wheels of the carriage on the slippery road and out of the four-inch deep mud that filled most of trail.

"Go you beasts, run like the devil himself," the driver shouted in a husky voice from high atop his perch. He raised the whip into the air and whirled its leather length over his head three times before bringing it forward and then quickly back with a loud snap.

"Faster, ha, faster," he continued to yell, "you won't rest tell we get there, now run." The driver cracked the whip once more over the horse's backside. The team of horses reacted to their master's voice and whip by pulling harder and harder against their load. Now came more snorting from mighty four legged beasts. It was all that they could do to keep their footing on such a treacherous road as this. You could see the steam rising off the backs of each animal as they continued to press on.

Suddenly, the coach hit a large stone in the road, causing it to jolt into the air and slide to one side.

"Hey, what's going on up there?" the passenger sticks his head out of the window and yells to his driver.

"Slow down, are you trying to kill us?" the passenger continued to shout.

John Wiseman pulled his head back into the coach and straightened himself in his seat. He tried to remain dignified, while being tossed about by the rough road.

"That damn fool," John muttered to himself, as he was thrown once again to the other side of the coach's compartment. He strained to right himself against the seat.

"Hold on Sir, brace yourself!" the driver yelled down to his passenger, "I don't think we're going to make this turn."

A large tree trunk had fallen across the trail, partially blocking the turn. The driver placed his feet firmly into the floor board of the coach, trying to gain the best leverage. He pulled back on the reins, trying to halt the speeding team of horses. He reaches down and grabs at the wooden brake handle mounted by the side of his seat. A wooden board is pushed forward against one of the wagon's wheels. The friction against the wheel did very little in slowing down the speeding coach. The coach leans heavily to the right as the driver tries to navigate the abrupt left turn.

"Come on you nags, hold your footing," the frustrated driver yells to his team of horses.

With strained muscles and mouths biting hard on their bit, the horses did what they could to maneuver through the turn.

Swinging much too wide, it was obvious that they would not be able to clear the fallen tree; the coach's right front wheel strikes a boulder along the side of the road. The wooden wheel splinters into several fragmented pieces and falls away from its axle. The carriage and its occupants are catapulted forward through the air for a short distance, sending the driver out of his seat and smashing to the ground. Amazingly the whole rig remains upright as it comes to a rest. The horses' stomp their feet in an unsettled manner, restless and scared, the beasts pace nervously in the mud.

Picking himself up from the ground, the driver struggles to stand; his pant leg is ripped open exposing a large four inch gash in his left leg that makes him squint with pain. Blood instantly begins to stream out of the wound. He quickly removes a length of rope from around his waist that up until now had been holding his baggy trousers, and wraps his leg with it. The rope tourniquet slows the blood flow. Now he must see to his team of horses. He manages to hobble over to the horses; they are extremely agitated by this turn of events.

"Here, here, settle down," the driver makes a clicking sound with his mouth, trying to calm the restless team of horses. He reaches into his coat pocket and retrieves several bits of cane sugar and feeds some to each of his animals. They eagerly lick the sweet treat from their master's hand.

"There you go, it's alright," he clicks his tongue once more.

"Calm down now, it's fine," he reassures them.

The pain in his leg is of little importance to the driver, he is more concerned with the welfare of his animals, besides, if something were to happen to the horses, it would be difficult to get to any sort of safety or shelter.

He untangles the leather reins and disconnects the lead line from the coach before securing the team of horses to a nearby tree limb.

"There ye go, that should hold ya," he says to the horses as he pats one of them on the side of the head.

Dragging his left foot behind, he walks back to the carriage, to check on the condition of his passenger.

The rain has finally stopped, leaving the entire area bathed in a fine mist, lit from the rising morning sun.

"Sir, Sir, are you alright in there? Oh, please forgive me Sir, I beg you."

John is lying on the floor of the buggy, having hit his head quite hard on the roof as he was thrown forward. He is otherwise unharmed.

He looks up at the driver, "My god man, I told you to mind your speed," John yells as he searches for his hat.

"Sir, let me help you," the little driver offers his assistance, but Mr. Wiseman puts his hand on the old man's shoulder and pushes him away.

"I don't need any help, leave me be," John crawls out of the coach and continues to chastise the driver.

"What in God's name did you think you were doing?" John asks, not really expecting any kind of answer, "So, how long will this delay us?"

"Not very long, good Sir, you may stand here to the side and I will get the wheel replaced as prompt as possible." The driver retrieves an umbrella from under the upper bench seat and offers it to his passenger.

"Here sir, this will keep you dry if it should begin to rain again," the driver says.

John accepts the umbrella, "Now get busy with the repair, I can't be delayed any longer then necessary," John replies.

He never asks about the welfare of his driver or even notices his blood drenched trousers, John cares very little for the needs of others. He worries only about himself and his needs and comforts.

John stood at the side of the road pulling and straightening at his jacket and grey pleated trousers. He was dressed in the finest attire of the day. John removes his fine silk hat, exposing his wavy black head of hair; he brushes a few small leaves from the brim of his hat before returning it to his head.

John was a very proper gentleman, both in attire and mannerism. He stood well over six feet and was of a slim build. It was very obvious to those around him that he had been raised with a silver spoon in his mouth. Yes, he presented the image of a very proper gentleman indeed. Unfortunately, he was not very proper, nor gentlemanly when it came to the way that he treated others. He seemed to think that all others were beneath him in both fortune and status.

"Well then, get to it man," John tells the driver.

The crippled driver went about his task of changing the wheel. Not once did John offer any kind of assistance to the poor man.

After retrieving two good solid branches from a nearby tree, the driver used these to form a y-support for the axle. He wedged the support into place and with the use of a wooden hammer the steel peg that held the remains of the old wheel to the axle was knocked free. A spare wheel was kept strapped to the underside of the coach. The driver hammered the new wheel onto the axial, at first it refused to move so he continued to hammer at the hub of the new wheel. Finally after much coaxing, the wooden wheel slid into place. The four-inch thick branches had managed to hold everything up, until the new wheel was secured with the steel peg. Now it was just a matter of knocking the branches away from the coach.

The driver raised his hammer and took one hard swing at the make shift wooden braces holding up the coach.

"There that should do it," the driver says as he steps back to briefly admire his work.

He turns back and hobbles off toward the team of horses. The driver reconnects the harness to the coach and makes sure that it is pulled tight and secure.

"At least you horses got some time to rest," he says to the beasts.

The little driver returns to the side of the road where John has been idly standing.

"Sir, if you are ready, you may get back into the carriage and we can be on our way again," the old driver said as he stowed the broken wheel and hammer in their proper places.

The rain had stopped completely as John made his way to the coach. He stopped and handed the umbrella to the driver.

"Here, take this. Do you think that we can avoid any further delays? I need to be on time," John remarks to the little man.

"We shall arrive in Favisham by late afternoon, I'll have you there in time for dinner Sir," offered the driver.

"Do you think that I care about dinner you fool? I need to be at my brother's side, before this day's sun sets," John says as he gives the driver a scornful look.

John pulled on a golden chain that was strung from his belt to a pocket in his vest. At the end of the chain was the finest jewel encrusted watch. Diamonds covered the front and back of the solid gold watchcase. John pressed the stem on the top of the watch and the cover dropped open with a click to expose a watch face made of mother of pearl. The numbers on the dial were highlighted with little rubies and other priceless gems. John notes the time and carefully closes the fine timepiece and returns it to his vest pocket.

As a youth, an uncle had left the watch to him at the time of his demise. This was an uncle that he had learned to hate while growing up under his guardianship. But now, here he was on a journey home to Favisham. A journey that started three long days ago, from just outside Liverpool.

The driver held the coach door as his passenger seated himself in the coach. John began to gather up a few of his belongings that had been thrown about during the rough ride. He threw a heavy wool blanket over his lap to keep the chill away and settled back into the bench for the remainder of his trip.

With a great deal of struggle, the old driver pulled himself up to the seat at the front of the coach. He grimaced as a sharp pain shot down the length of his leg. He would surely need to see a doctor the first chance that he gets. But for now he must endure the pain.

The driver grabs hold of the reins.

"Ha, ha, let's go now," the driver yelled to his team of horses.

A solid crack of the driver's whip and they were once again on their way.

* CHAPTER TWO *

John watched as the mountain scenery, with its green rolling hills, streamed past his window. The morning sun, now shinning bright, swept its way across the valley, bathing it in a golden glow. The rhythmic sound of the horse's hooves pounding into the dirt road in unison lulled John into a dreamy like state.

John found himself recalling why he was on this journey to begin with. It had all started just a few days back.

It was late afternoon and John was working at his office desk in Liverpool, he owned a small, but successful accounting firm. He made enough money to live a fairly comfortable life, but that meant that he was always hard at work. Many a night John would sleep in his office, it had become as much of a home to him as anywhere. He didn't have much of a social life because of his obsession with work.

Breaking the silence of John's concentration, Miss Marbel, his secretary, came bursting into his office. She shuffled her stubby little feet as she walked, this had always annoyed John.

"I beg your pardon Sir, I don't mean to disturb you, but a wire gram has just been delivered for you," she says in her high pitched voice, "I think it is from your brother, Trulane. The postmark is from Favisham. Shall I open it for you Sir?

John snatched the paper from her hand.

"Is your name on this? Get out. Get back to work," he commands his employee.

Miss Marbel turned her stout little frame towards the door as she went to leave.

"Well I never," she says as she slams the office door behind her.

John stands behind his big oak desk as he reads the message on the paper. The wire is not from his brother, but rather, from his brother's butler, Mr. Quince.

John sits down in his big leather chair and begins to read:

"Master John Wiseman,
    Sir, please come at once. You are needed at Favisham Castle. Your brother Trulane is deathly ill.
    Please hurry."

The letter was simply signed:

"Mr. Quince."

There was no mention of the kind of illness that Trulane had developed, nor how such a thing had happened. There was just the dire request to come to his brother's side.

It had been five years, since John last visited his boyhood home in Favisham. He wasted very little time that afternoon. After making arrangements to cover his absence from the office, John secured his transportation; he would be traveling from Liverpool to Favisham by horse drawn coach. He would depart later that evening.

"Ha, ha, run you nags," the sound of the Driver's voice, startled John from his daydream.

John shook the fogginess from his head and focused on the passing scenery once more. The sun was high in the sky now and John could see little villages and their houses scattered about the hillside. All of the houses had the same slanted, brown thatch roof and from a distance they all looked exactly the same. Some of the houses had rows of terraces carved into the hillside behind them. These terraces were used to farm the hilly terrain. This part of the country was not suited for farming and so it made for a very difficult life. Favisham was very much like this. The big difference being that John and his brother had been raised in Favisham Castle and not a lowly village hut. Those houses were for the common people.

John pulled his prize watch from his pocket and checked the time. It was now, well past two in the afternoon.

"Hey, you up there, driver," John called out as he rapped his fist against the roof of the carriage.

"Hey, I say can you hear me?" John called out once again trying to get the drivers attention.

The team of horses gradually began to slow the coach to a walk.

"Is there a problem Sir?" asked the driver as he leaned down on the brake lever.

"Pull up to that INN, so I may get something to eat," John motioned in the direction of a small group of buildings off on a narrow side road.

"Yes Sir, right away Sir."

The driver cracked his whip and pointed the team of horses in the proper direction.

The carriage stopped at the INN and John jumped out of the back.

"You stay out here and mind the horses; I'll bring you something to eat when I am done. I can't be seen eating with someone like you," with that, John went about fussing with his hat and coat, trying to knock three days worth of road dirt from his clothes.

"Yes Sir, I'll stay here with the horses and coach. What ever you ask, good Sir." There was definitely the tone of resentment in the driver's voice and once John was well out of sight, the little driver made some sort of hand motion in the direction of his very rude passenger.

14

The driver waited for what seemed like an hour or more. Meanwhile, inside the little pub, John was taking his time, gorging himself on soup, bread and ale. He sat at the far end of the room as he ate, after having his fill John summoned the barkeep to his table.

"What is my bill?" he asked of the elderly looking man.

The old barkeep stood silent as he was trying to figure up the amount in his head.

John had no time for this delay; he reached into his vest pocket and produced two small gold coins.

"Here, this should cover it," John said as he tossed the two pieces of precious metal onto the table.

"Yes, yes, thank you Sir," the old man said as he scooped up the coins.

"Wrap this up for me," John said as he pushed his plate toward the old barkeeper.

John exited the tavern and returned to his waiting coach.

"Here, I brought you a little to eat," John handed a small bundled napkin to the driver and climbed back into the carriage.

"Oh, thank you Sir, very nice of you Sir," the driver eagerly unwrapped his prize as he thanked John for the food.

Unfortunately, all that was in the napkin were a few large crumbs of bread, obviously leftovers. The driver stuffed the small morsels into his mouth. He retrieved a small metal flask of ale that he kept strapped to his vest and washed down the dry bread.

"Are you just going to sit here? Let's be on our way," John yelled to his driver. "I must be in Favisham before night fall."

The driver quickly drank the remainder of his ale, tilting his head back to savor every last drop. He then secured the flask under his coat for safekeeping.

"Yes Sir, right away Sir, I'll have you there before dark."

Once again the coach was on the road, making its way to the village of Favisham and the castle home of Trulane Wiseman.

* CHAPTER THREE *

As the day wore on, the coach ride seemed to be endless. John found himself daydreaming of his boyhood home at Favisham. He had left this place many years ago, to escape the almost iron grip it had on his life. This place, with all of its memories, had hardly been a loving home to John. At the first opportunity that presented itself, John was quick to seek his freedom, while his older brother Truelane chose to stay behind and live in Favisham Castle.

Trulane and John had been orphaned early in life. John was three years younger than Trulane, but seemed to be the wiser of the two. Their mother had died at a very young age; she suffered during complications giving birth to John. Phillip Wiseman, their father, had tried to do his best at raising the two boys on his own.

Phillip ran a small import export business that required him to travel. He would be forced to leave the boys for many weeks on end. Many of his travels took him to far off exotic places around the world. Mr. Quince would take care of the boys at those times and see to the needs of the household. They lived quite a comfortable life, for a while.

That life came to an end late one evening as the boys received news that their father had been murdered and robbed while returning from a business trip in Liverpool. The police constable in Favisham had delivered the shocking news to the family butler Mr. Quince. The constable assembled the two boys and Mr. Quince at the big round table that sat in the Wiseman entry hall.

"Good Sirs, I have some very tragic news. Your Father has been murdered, he was attacked last evening in the city," said Constable Perry.

Mr. Quince stood closer to the boys, an arm around each one of them.

"No!" cried little John as he began to sob.

"Be strong, be strong," Mr. Quince hugs the boys more closely as he says this.

"It grieves me to have to tell you such news, be assured that we are studying the case and gathering evidence. We are trying to find any clue that would help us. However, it is quite likely that we will never find your father's killer. We really don't have very much to go on," the constable went on to say, "I am so very sorry."

The older of the two boys, Trulane, managed to hold back the tears that were on the verge of running down his cheeks.

Looking up at Mr. Quince, he says, "Papa promised me that he would be home for my birthday tomorrow."

Mr. Quince has trouble holding his own emotions in check and does not reply.

The boys were visibly shaken by such news. Mr. Quince did his best to comfort them.

"You must be strong young men now, the way your father would have wanted," he tells them.

"I'm so sorry to be the one to have to tell you this," continued the constable, feeling rather uncomfortable, "but, you will have to go and live with one of your relatives. You can no longer stay hear in this house. An adult must be put in charge of your upbringing and be responsible for your welfare. Your father's brother has agreed to take you in. It would seem that your only living relative is your Uncle Richard."

The two boys looked at each other in total disbelief. Their Uncle Richard had always been so mean to the both of them. Even their father had very little to do with Richard. Richard had married into a very rich, land owning family. He always made it clear to everyone that he was better then they were.

"Is there no other choice Sir?" inquired Trulane.

"I'm sorry. This is the only arrangement available to you," responded the constable.

Even Mr. Quince objected to the situation. "Surely you can't believe that Sir Richard would have the boys' best interest at heart. He is by far the most heartless and selfish man to ever live here in Favisham."

"That is why I have arranged for you to live at the castle with the boys and see to their needs," Responded Constable Perry.

This bit of added news helped to belay some of the boys' fears. At least Mr. Quince would be there with them.

The Constable stood to leave; "You have two days to get all of your affairs in order, at which time I will return to take you to Favisham Castle. Good day."

"Two days? Sir that will just not do. I have much to take care of in preparing for such a drastic move. Surely you might allow us more time then that," asked Mr. Quince.

"I'm sorry sir, but those are the orders of the court. I will see you in two days," the constable said as he made his exit.

That is how the two Wiseman boys had come to live at Favisham Castle.

In John's youth, he had toiled long and hard to try and please his uncle, but that was never the case. All he ever seemed to do was to aggravate and disappoint. Trulane, on the other hand, could do no wrong in his uncle's eyes. Uncle Richard heaped praise and adoration on Trulane and John got criticism and scorn.

When in school, both John and Trulane participated in sports such as track and other field events. John might finish in the top three and Trulane in the bottom, Trulane would get rewarded for his effort and John would get scolded for not finishing first. His Uncle Richard went out of his way to make life tough. Leaving that place was the best thing that he had ever done.

"Woe there, woe," called out the driver.

The little old man let out a shrill whistle as he slowed the team of horses and brought the coach to a stop just outside of the main gate to Favisham Castle.

The grand thirty room house stood high on a hill, it was surrounded by weed choked gardens and fountains that had rusted and stopped flowing years ago. There was a large mermaid perched high on top of one of the fountains. A long time ago, John remembers how water would spray from the bottle that she held in her out-stretched hands. Her hands were now missing and her tail was broken off half way up. It had been a long time since any water ran through the old fountain. The only water that it contained now was a stagnant pool of green slime in it's' basin. Everything seemed to be in a sad state of disrepair.

A ten-foot high stone wall ran the perimeter of the property. The wall had been built by the original owners to protect them from land robbers and to keep the lowly village people separated from the ruling elite class. Wild climbing weeds and thick chocking brush had overtaken the wall. One could hardly make out the rough hewn stone that lay beneath the heavy over growth.

John had drifted off to sleep for the best part of two hours. Now, after waking to these sights, John's head was still awash in a daze of painful memories. His boyhood memories quickly began to fade as he pulled himself up in his seat and slowly started to regain his wits.

"Maybe I can find something good to remember about this place", John thought to himself.

John continued to look over the sprawling un-kept landscape of Favisham Estates. He hadn't noticed how dreary or foreboding the atmosphere had become. A thickness seemed to surround everything in a yellowish foul smelling fog. John recognized the distasteful aroma as that of sulfur, choking thick sulfur. You could literally feel it in your lungs as you struggled to take in the vile air.

John wondered what this all could mean. He continued to focus his eyes on the now strange surroundings as best as he could. The light was now gone from the day and nothing but darkness swallowed the senses.

John felt the coach beginning to slow as it approached the driveway that led to a large towering gate.

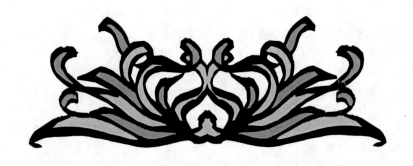

* CHAPTER FOUR *

"Sir, we are here. Just waiting for the doorman to come down to the road and open the gate for us," the driver yelled from his perch.

After a few moments, John could see the figure of a man dressed all in pale blue velvet, and wearing a tri-cornered hat with a long feather plume. The feather was very worn and bent at its center. The strange figure of a man came down the long winding road that led from the Castle. The man walked with a wide stride in both length and girth. Clutched in his left hand was a large metal ring about four inches in diameter, two large bronze keys were threaded onto the ring and they clanged and jingled as the man walked. John remembered the man's name as; Jarvis Garwood, he had worked for the Wiseman family for nearly forty years. It had always been his job to see to any visitors that approached the large gate and give them access to the main entrance of the grounds, and once they had been announced to the master of the house, then and only then were they allowed to proceed any further.

Jarvis said not a word to the visitors at the gate, but went about his task. He fumbled with the large key ring, selecting one of the keys. He inserted the key into a half rusted slot, thus removing the big iron lock, which held the gate closed.

The blue velvet man stepped to the side of the cobblestone drive and made a motion with his left hand for the coach to proceed up to the castle. Jarvis then closed the gate and secured it once more with the giant iron lock. After making sure that all was well, Jarvis went to stand guard in a little building just off to the side of the huge gate. This had been his station for most of his life, watching the entrance and maintaining the gate to Favisham Castle.

The driver stopped the coach at the foot of the great marble steps that flanked the front of the building. Four giant torches blazed against the dark sky, they lined the marble staircase, casting a bright orange glow to the steps and the stone front of the castle.

The thick smell of sulfur continued to sting at Johns' lungs with every breath that he struggled to take.

John pulled his jeweled watch from his vest pocket and noted that the time was just shortly after eight P.M. The trip had taken longer than he had expected. He returned the watch to his pocket and proceeded to exit the coach.

"Please see to my bags," he barked his order at the tired old driver.

"Yes Sir, right away sir."

The driver wasted little time unloading the two large travel cases that were strapped to the back of the coach. He followed closely behind John.

John walked up the steps and was met by Mr. Quince at the front door.

"Good to see you Sir, have your man leave those bags there in the hall. I will see to them later. Now please, right this way," Mr. Quince made a sweeping motion with his hand.

Mr. Quince was a short round man with silver hair all neatly pulled back in a tight knot and ponytail. A small green ribbon tied neatly at the back of his head, held it all in place; this was the style of the day. He was dressed in a black suit with waistcoat and short pants. A white ruffled shirt completed the ensemble. He was a very proper man servant.

"After you stable and feed your team of horses, have the cook make you something to eat. You must be very hungry after a long day of travel," Mr. Quince addresses the old driver.

"Thank you good Sir, you are too kind," he replies.

"I see that you have wounded your leg, do you require a doctor?" asks Mr. Quince as he has noticed the tourniquet wound about the drivers leg.

"No Sir, I'm sure that after some food and rest, I shall be fine. Thank you for your concern and hospitality," says the driver.

"It would be no problem; I could have a doctor take a look at that for you. There is a doctor in the house right now, shall I have him take a look at that?" asks Mr. Quince.

"Again, thank you sir, but I shall be fine with a little rest. Your kindness is appreciated," the driver says as he finishes stacking the travel bags in a neat pile.

John and Mr. Quince leave the driver to see to the bags and head off down a long corridor.

Mr. Quince led the way through the house and up the stairs to John's old room at the end of the grand hallway.

"I hope you don't mind Sir, but I thought that you might like to stay here in your old boyhood room while you are staying at Favisham," Mr. Quince says.

They enter a large oak walled room that has very little furniture, just a bed with a night stand, a few chairs by a table and a stack of wood by the fireplace.

Mr. Quince begins to place a few of John's personal items into the drawer of the bed table. John is pacing the room.

John wasted no time, "How is my brother? Has his condition grown worse?" the tone in John's voice was urgent.

"I heard you tell my driver that the doctor was still here, what is Trulane's' condition? What is it that you are not telling me? I must talk to the doctor at once and I want to see my dear brother. I traveled all of this distance to be at his side," John said with a bit of frustration in his voice.

"Sir, the Doctor has just left Trulane's side; he waits for you in the sitting room. Perhaps you would like to freshen up. I will tell the good doctor that you shall be with him shortly."

"Yes, that will do," John replied as Mr. Quince left the room.

Doctor Raymond, a tall grey haired man wearing a pair of spectacles, finished packing his medical instruments into the small black bag that was always at his side. He got up from his sitting room chair and began to pace back and forth. He was obviously upset about his patient.

John finished putting on fresh clothes and left his room. He descended the great oak stairway and entered the sitting room.

"So, tell me Doctor Raymond, what is my brothers' condition?" John asked.

"Please take a seat and I will try and explain," the Doctor pointed to a chair.

"I didn't travel all of this way to take a seat. Tell me now, without all of the drama." John was stern and had little patients for anyone.

"What is wrong with Trulane and how serious is this illness that I should be summoned to his side? I demand to see my brother, what is his condition?" John questioned.

"Sir, I am afraid that it is quite serious. Your brother is dying," the Doctor announced.

John started for the door, "I must see him, I must go to him now."

"No. I have given him a heavy sedative. He is resting now. You can see him in the morning," the doctor informed him.

John walked over to the window and stood looking at his own reflection "What is wrong with him?" he asked.

"I wish that I could answer that Sir," responded the Doctor, "His illness is unknown to the medical world. I have consulted all of my medical books and have tried several treatments. His condition still grows worse. Most of his body functions have begun to shut down. He is simply dying sir. All that can be done is to make him as comfortable as possible for the few remaining days that he has."

"What are you saying? How long does he have?" asked John, still staring out the window.

"Sir, it can be hard to say," the doctor replies.

John turned sharply from the window. "How long?" he repeated. His eyes were ablaze by this time.

"Maybe a day, possibly two days, he is wasting away and growing weaker by the minute. I will stop in on you in the morning. I must be going. I have yet another stop to make tonight."

"So, that's it then? Just like that, I am supposed to except that my brother only has perhaps days to live? This will not do, you will not leave his side until he is cured, and I do not care what other patients you have to see this evening, my brother's life is surely more important then the life of some lowly villager." John was so caught up in his own world that nothing was more important then the needs of his brother.

"I'm sorry that you feel that way Sir," the doctor said as he continued to gather his things.

"There is absolutely nothing that can be done for your brother at this point. The best thing that you could do is to see to his basic needs and try to make him as comfortable as possible in these last few days. Perhaps there are financial matters and wills to go over?" Doctor Raymond tried to explain things to John, "Please Mr. Wiseman," he continued, "you must come to terms with the fact that your brother will die in a very short time, I wish that there was more that I could do for Trulane, but alas it is not to be. I had hoped for some sort of change after the medication that I administered the other day. I am very sorry Sir. I do have other patients that need my assistance this evening. Again, I am very sorry."

John said nothing more as Doctor Raymond retrieved his black bag from large maple table and left the room. Mr. Quince escorted Dr. Raymond to the front of the house. The Doctor got his hat and coat from Mr. Quince, who was standing ready at the door in the foyer.

"I am sure that Mr. Wiseman did not mean to be so rude and abrupt with you tonight, he is having a very tough time coming to grips with this," said Mr. Quince.

"Yes I realize that, perhaps you can help him to understand," the doctor offered.

"I will do my best Sir," says the man servant of the house.

"I will return in the morning, but I really do not expect that there will be any change in Trulane's condition. Good evening Sir," Doctor Raymond says his final farewell and leaves the confines of Favisham Castle and steps swiftly down the steep marble steps at the front of the estate.

* CHAPTER FIVE *

John waited to hear the big oak doors close behind the good Doctor. He turned back to the window once more. He stood watching until the Doctor had boarded his coach and was on his way down the road and out the front gate. Jarvis, the blue velvet man secured the big lock on the gate and returned to his little two-room guard post.

John stood at the window for several minutes, his eyes focused into the distance while his mind drifted off to some unknown place. Just as John turned away from the window, something caught his eye. There was a strange shape on the other side of the road and it was heading for the front gate. John could not make out the shape, at first it appeared to be some sort of green smoke, its size continued to swirl and grow.

John watched as this mysterious thing moved up to the gate.

"Surely Jarvis would notice such a thing as this," John found himself thinking.

The figure moved right up to the gate. John could see its' swirling mass through the iron bars of the gate. It paused for a moment and then seemed to melt right through the metal bars. It was growing bigger now, much bigger then a man and its features seemed to shift in the dark of the night.

John turned his gaze away from this sight for a moment and rubbed his eyes with both hands. He looked back out of the window to see if Jarvis had seen the intruder come through the gate. There was no movement from inside the guard shack; John could just make out the silhouette of Jarvis as he sat by his lamp in the little building. Jarvis had not heard or seen a thing.

John stood transfixed on the sight, afraid to turn away.

"What is this thing?" he muttered.

The aberration moved straight ahead as if it had a sense of purpose to its movements. The shape continued to grow and take on form as it advanced up the steps to the house. John lost sight of the object for a few moments. He left the window and ran to the door of the room. He stuck his head out into the hallway.

"Mr. Quince, Mr. Quince, come at once. I need you to see something," John called out. He needed another pair of eyes to witness this thing, whatever it was.

Mr. Quince had been out in the kitchen cooking a late meal for Master John. He put down the plate that he was preparing and hurried to the sitting room.

"Yes sir, what is it sir?"

"Come here to the window, quick, take a look at this," John turned for a brief moment, just long enough to wave Mr. Quince to the window.

Alas, when John turned back to the window, the figure had vanished. Not a sign remained.

"Damn, it's gone," John said.

"What was it Sir?" asked Mr. Quince.

"Must be my eyes playing tricks on me. I thought for sure that there was something or someone out there." John rubbed his eyes; "Perhaps I'm just tired after my journey."

"I'm sure after you have a little bite to eat and a good nights sleep, you'll feel much better in the morning and then you can see your brother Trulane," assures Mr. Quince.

"Yes, very well, perhaps you are right," added John.

"If you will follow me into the kitchen Sir, I have prepared a hearty bowl of vegetable stew for you," said Mr. Quince.

John walked several paces behind the man servant. Mr. Quince pulled a chair out from the table and motioned for John to be seated and then went about spooning up a large serving of stew into a wooden bowl. Mr. Quince sat the bowl in front of John along with a small biscuit and a glass of water.

"There you are Sir, I know that it is not much, but on such short notice..."

"No, this is just fine Mr. Quince," John interrupted.

Mr. Quince bowed a bit at his master.

"Please Mr. Quince, I must ask you a few questions, won't you come and sit here with me at the table?" John said.

The old man servant sat with his master at the table but still tried to stay in his place as a servant.

"What has happened here? John wanted to know.

"Why is the house and property in such a sad state of disrepair? I was appalled at what I saw as I drove up to the front of the house."

"Yes Sir I know what you mean, you have not been here in quite a long time and a lot has changed. You see after your brother's wife died, he lost all interest in anything. One might say that he even lost his will to live at all. He dismissed most of the servants and grounds keepers. There is just Jarvis at the gate, a stable boy to watch after the few horses that remain and finally myself. I have done all that I can do to keep the castle running."

"I don't blame you Mr. Quince; I am surely in your debt for all that you have done for me and my family. It was just such a shock to the system to return to this place after such a long absence and find that the once grand estate of Favisham should have changed this much. Tell me Mr. Quince, when did Trulane fall so ill?"

John slurped the last few spoonfuls of soup into his mouth and waited to here Mr. Quinces' reply.

"Like I told you, he fell into such a deep depression for the better part of two years and then it seemed for a brief time that he was going to snap out of it and get on with his life and that was when this mysterious illness took hold of your brother," Mr. Quince paused for a moment and took a sip from his glass of water.

"I know how hard this must be for you Sir, but we must be strong," the servant added.

"I hope that Trulane will be awake in the morning, I really need to talk to him I need to let him know that I am here and will not leave his side until the time that he recovers," John said.

"Master John, the Doctor has told you that your brother is not going to live much longer. Why do you continue to not face the facts?" asked Mr. Quince.

"I will not believe it until I see and talk to Trulane. How can there be no answer or cure for his illness?" John raised his voice slightly as he demanded some sort of answer.

"I wish that I had an answer for you Sir, but alas such things are beyond my realm of knowledge," Mr. Quince responded, "perhaps things will improve in the morning and the tide will turn in Trulane's favor." Mr. Quince knew that this would not be the case but wanted to give some hope to John even if it was unfounded.

Mr. Quince got up from the table and began to clear the dishes and placed them in the big kettle of wash water by the wood burning stove.

"You really should be getting some rest now sir, I will see to these dishes in the morning."

"Yes, you are right Mr. Quince, it has been a very long day for me, and in the morning everything will be clear. So if you will excuse me, I will head off to my room."

"I will walk with you up the stairs sir," said Mr. Quince.

The two of them made their way up the steep flight of stairs to the second floor landing. After a brief goodnight the two men headed off in separate directions. John was lost in thought as he made his way to his upstairs bedroom.

* CHAPTER SIX *

Later that evening;

"If that will be all Sir, I will see you in the morning, I bid you good night," Mr. Quince bowed slightly and closed the door to John's room. He went off down the hallway to his own sleeping quarters. It had been a long day for Mr. Quince.

John was a little confused as to what he had seen outside the castle gate. Was it just his weary eyes playing tricks, as Mr. Quince had suggested? Perhaps a good nights sleep would clear his mind. He would go to his brother's side in the morning.

Putting on his nightgown, John readied himself for bed. He laid his trousers and shirt neatly across a chair, running his fingers through the pockets of his pants; he retrieves his jeweled watch and sets it on the small table next to his bed.

That jeweled watch was the only thing that John had gotten at the time of his Uncle Richards death. His Uncle's will had laid out the terms of his inheritance, the two boys, John and Trulane, after reaching the age of twenty, would have to leave Favisham Castle unless they were to marry and agree to stay in Favisham for the rest of their lives. John had other plans, and they did not involve staying in Favisham. He wanted to get as far away as he could, away from all of the cruel memories that haunted him in this place.

Trulane had met a young girl named Elisabeth Stroud, they fell deeply in love and were married, it was his dream to stay at the castle and start a family. That dream had been cut short for Trulane; his young wife had died giving birth to a baby that unfortunately also did not survive. The loss of his true love Elisabeth had deeply saddened Trulane, after that he had more or less become a recluse and shut in at Favisham Castle.

On the day that John announced his plans to leave Favisham, the family's lawyer, Mr. Cransten presented him with a small old leather box, and he told John that this was one item that his Uncle Richard had left only to him.

"What is it?" John wanted to know.

He reached out with both hands and took the small box from Mr. Cransten. John sat the old container on the table in front of him and paused before continuing. He sat there starring at the small prize in front of him.

"What special thing could Uncle Richard had left, that was just for him?" John wondered.

John opened the old box very slowly and was amazed at what he saw inside. Inside the red velvet lined box was the most beautiful, jewel covered watch that he had ever seen, along with a brief hand written note from his Uncle Richard.

John held the watch dangling from its long golden chain. John was mesmerized by this beautiful piece of craftsmanship. The watch was truly a work of art.

John unfolded the small letter that was also in the box and began to read the scribbled handwriting; he instantly recognized the bold stylish strokes on the page as that of his despised Uncle Richard.

A slight shiver ran the length of his spine as he began to read;

"Dear John,

As you are reading this letter, it must have been your decision to leave Favisham for good. I have instructed Mr. Cransten to give this gift to you. This is one way that I hope to repay you for all the misery I must have put you through as a child. I saw a little too much of myself in you, and it disturbed me. Have a wonderful life.

Yours truly,
Richard
Wiseman."

"That's it?" John remembered thinking at the time.

After the childhood that old man had put him through, did he really think that this little trinket was supposed to make up for that?

John took a long deep breath and shook those memories from his head. He was back in the here and now.

John took one more look at his precious watch and then climbed into the large overstuffed bed. He settled his head back into the thick feather pillow and tried to calm himself down after the long day's journey.

The night air was cold as John pulled the covers up over his head, trying to stop the chills that shock him from head to toe. The old castle was still as drafty and damp as it had been in his youth, always fighting off the bone numbing cold by adding more wood to the huge furnace and fireplaces throughout the house. Tonight was no different; John pulled himself from the bed and crossed the room to get more wood for the fireplace in his bedroom. He selected three large pieces of wood and bundled them into his arms, struggling with his load; John was crossing in front of his bedroom window, when something startled him.

"OH MY GOD! WHAT, what do you want?" John yelled as he dropped the heavy wood to the ground, sending splinters scattering across the cold floor, and just missing his foot with the largest log.

John fell to his knees, looking up at the window, "What are you? Go away, leave me alone," John was shaking with fright unable to move.

The face that starred back at him from outside the window was not the face of anything human. The hooded figure had Yellow demon eyes that glared out from bleached bone sockets. What little bit of flesh that remained on what was apparently its face hung in a dripping mass from its skull. A black tongue thrashed from side to side in a ragged whole where a mouth and jaw might have been. Low, non-human sounds came from the creature's throat.

"Please go away," John whimpered.

The thing at the window made a gesture with one of its gloved hands. It tapped at the glass a few times and tried to point at something in the room. The thing was trying to say something, but had no jaw with which to form the words. It wanted John to see something.

Again it tapped at the glass and pointed in the direction of the far wall of John's room. There was a very large portrait of Trulane hanging in the middle of the wall. John looked at the picture for a moment. He wasn't sure what it was that this thing was trying to show him.

Then, in a flash it was clear. John turned his gaze back to the hideous face at the window. The grotesque thing seemed to be smiling with its eyes as it nodded at John with its hooded head.

"No, you will not take my brother this night, I will not allow you to have him," John manages to get up on his feet.

"I know who you are now; I've heard stories all my life, YOU ARE THE GATE KEEPER!"

John points a finger at the image; "You will not doom my brother to the same fate."

A low gutted sound came from what was once the mouth of the GateKeeper, John was just able to make out the words;

"Tomorrow I shall return for the one called Trulane, but tonight I must take the soul of another to the grave. A young girl on the other side of town will be my target tonight."

John stepped back from the window, and watched as the apparition of the GateKeeper faded into a green mist, and then was gone.

This was the thing that John had seen earlier outside of the castle gate. He was sure that this thing was real and not a figment of his over stressed mind as Mr. Quince had suggested.

John was sure that this hideous creature was here to take Trulane.

Stumbling back across the room, John sat himself down in the big leather chair next to his bed. He recalled the stories behind the legend of the GateKeeper. It had been told through the generations in these parts, that when someone dies and is laid to rest in the city cemetery, his soul is trapped in the graveyard until another person is buried, and that soul replaces him, allowing him to leave its earthly bounds. Until such time, he is doomed to walk the grounds of the cemetery and keep watch over the gate to the dead. Those that are about to die or those that are about to lose someone very close, see the GateKeeper.

"I will not let him take my brother," John snaps out of his stupor. He jumps up and grabs his dressing robe. As he puts one arm through the sleeve he is already reaching for the doorknob and heading out into the hall.

"Sir, what is all of the commotion? I heard what sounded like a howl coming from your room," Mr. Quince was racing down the hall as he spoke. He came face to face with John.

"What is it sir?" He asked as he pulled at his belt, closing his robe.

"I've seen it, it was here," John put a hand on each of Mr. Quince's shoulders, "Listen I tell you, the Gate Keeper, the GateKeeper was here. He was at my window howling a threat."

"Are you sure Sir? Mr. Quince took this information very seriously. He too, had once seen the GateKeeper. He was only a child at the time, but that very day, was the day that his father would die.

"He will return tomorrow for Trulane. Please what can we do?" John was looking to Mr. Quince for any glimmer of hope.

"Sir, I fear that your brother's time is short and there is really very little that can be done for him." Mr. Quince tried his best to console John.

"I must go to my brothers' side at once," John moved his way around Mr. Quince and headed down the hall to Trulane's room. He sensed that the loss of his brother's very soul might be at stake on this most troublesome night.

* CHAPTER SEVEN*

The room was almost dark as John opened the heavy wooden door to Trulane's bedroom. John stepped back as a claustrophobic feeling suddenly came over him. John took a deep breath and entered the room. The air in the bedroom was moist and thick from the water that was boiling over the fireplace; the doctor had added some inhalant to the water that was supposed to help Trulane to breathe easier. Two small candles flickered in silent vigil by the head of the bed. The atmosphere was of waiting death.

John walked to the edge of his brother's bed and was startled to see that Trulane's eyes were wide open and starring at the ceiling of his room. He didn't seem to be aware of John's presence by his side. John was shocked by the sight of his brother; he looked so pale and thin and most of his dark head of hair had fallen out and left Trulane looking twenty years older. This was not the way John had expected to find his brother. He had always been the picture of health and vigor. John leaned closer to his dying brother and began to speak softly into Trulane's left ear, perhaps he could get through to him.

"Trulane, Trulane can you hear me?" John touched the arm of his brother; it was ice cold and clammy.

"Please brother, can you hear me?" pleaded John.

Just as John touched Trulane's arm a second time, Trulane sat straight up in his bed and with one hand reached out and grabbed Johns arm in a vice like grip.

"The GateKeeper, I saw it, he's coming for me," Trulane shouted.

John was truly startled by this sudden outburst he jerked his arm away from Trulane.

"Don't let me be the last one in the graveyard, please promise. No matter what, you must not let me be the last one buried," Trulane looked into John's eyes, this was the first time that he had actually acknowledged the fact that John was even in the room with him.

Trulane asked for his sworn promise.

"I will, dear brother, I will," John stroked his brother's hand as he spoke.

Trulane eased back down onto his bed and fell back into his drug-induced sleep.

"It is better that he rest Sir," Mr. Quince added from the doorway.

John had not been aware that Mr. Quince had been standing in the hall.

"The doctor will be returning in the morning, perhaps he can do something for your brother. We must not give up hope Sir."

"Yes, I know. But I will not leave my brothers side this night. You may go on to bed if you must, I will stand guard here tonight."

"If the GateKeeper comes, I am afraid that there is nothing that you will be able to do. I fear that will not be able to stop him from taking his next victim," Mr. Quince added.

"Yes, but I must try and protect him, I don't know how, but I must at least stay at his side," John replied.

"Do what you feel that you must. I will just be right down the hall if you should need me during the night. I will prey for your brother before I turn in," Mr. Quince said as he placed a hand on John's shoulder.

"I have never been one to believe in the power of prayer, but if you feel like that is all that you can do, then please go right ahead. We will need the help to keep the evil Gatekeeper at bay," John said as he put his own hand on top of Mr. Quinces hand and removed it from his shoulder.

"I will not leave my brother's side on this night."

"Very well Sir, but please try to get yourself some rest if you can," said Mr. Quince.

"Thank you, I will try. You should go now."

John ushered Mr. Quince out to the hall and said his good nights once again. He returned to Trulane's bedroom and took a seat in an oversized chair at the side of his brother's bed and covered himself against the cold with the extra blanket that lay there.

* CHAPTER EIGHT *

The only light in the room came from the few candles that were lit and the glow of the small fireplace. Its flames danced shadows of light and dark against the walls, creating a picture show of the bizarre.

John tried to ignore the shapes that danced around the room. He shifted uncomfortably in his chair. The shadows seemed to tease at John's fears; every shape took on that of the GateKeeper. John tried to tell himself that these things were just imaginary. John was determined to watch over his brother, he would do what he could to protect him.

Sliding his chair closer to Trulane's bed, John tried to stretch out his lanky legs by propping them up on the bed rail. He was close enough to hear his brothers labored breathing, his gasping at life, and the moans of a man about to die, perhaps.

John reached over and touched his brother's hand, "sleep, brother, I will watch over you tonight," he said.

And so, John sat in that big leather chair, into the wee hours of the night. It's funny how the lack of sleep can play tricks on ones senses. On several occasions, John caught himself nodding off. As his head dropped forward, it would jolt him back awake. John tried sitting up more rigid in the chair to see if he could make himself so uncomfortable as to not fall asleep again. John would fight off the need for sleep, as long as he could, but the flickering figures on the walls and ceiling started their dance in his head once again.

At some point during the night, sleep got the better of him and he was lost in his own world of nightmares. The veil of slumber and dark tortured dreams had taken over.

Strange souls, and rotting corpses, filled John's dream world with a kaleidoscope of terror. His body would twist and turn in the chair, trying to escape the creatures of his subconscious mind.

The nightmares and dreams had gotten the best of John; in his sleeping mind, John was about to be taken by some hideous creature. He screamed out loud in his sleep, this was enough to stir John out of his troubled slumber.

Slowly, ever so slowly back into the real world.

Opening one eye and then the other, John began to awake.

He sat in the chair for a moment, trying to shake off his disorientation. At about that time, John realized that he had fallen asleep, leaving his brother unguarded, he also realized that they were not alone in the room, that there was something terribly wrong, and John felt very uneasy. He truly sensed something evil in the room with him and Trulane.

John started to move from the chair, suddenly there was a strange sensation or rather a lack of sensation in John's entire body. Something was wrong, he was totally paralyzed, frozen to the chair.

Unable to move any part of his body, he tried to call out to Mr. Quince, but alas, no sound came out of John's throat and mouth. He was utterly trapped, unable to move or speak. With his eyes wide open and unblinking, John was about to become the unwilling witness to the taking of his brother's soul.

The room had the feel of death. The only sound that John was aware of was that of his own heart pounding in his ears and chest. A creeping mist of blue and green smoke materialized across the floor and began swirling around the room, becoming thicker and thicker. Once again the foul smell of sulfur and rot filled John's nostrils. It was by far the worst smell he had ever experienced.

A form began to congeal in the mist, and rise up higher in the room as it continued its whirling path. The pounding of John's heart was now deafening. His eyes fixed in their sockets, John watched in horror as the form took on a more familiar and sinister shape. The horrid thing stood at the foot of Trulane's bed, its yellow dead eyes, starred directly at John.

"The GateKeeper!" John screamed the name in his head.

The grotesque creature seemed to look right into John's very being, filling John with a sickening awareness. Beads of sweat streamed down his forehead and stung at John's frozen eyes, which now had the look of shear panic and freight.

The GateKeeper turned its stare toward Trulane, who was lying motionless on the bed. The creature let out a blood-curdling howl and was on top of Trulane in an instant. The thing straddled Trulane's body with its bony legs and sat down on his chest. Trulane's breathing became more labored. The GateKeeper lowered its own rotting head down closer to that of Trulane's. John could only watch with frightful terror, the GateKeeper's face was even more hideous then John had remembered. Discolored flesh hung from tendons and bone in a mocking resemblance of something that was once human.

The beast paused a moment and shot a glance in John's direction as if to make sure that John was watching him. As it leaned down, it licked at Trulane's face with that ever-present black thrashing tongue. The GateKeeper sat up straight and howled once again. He looked like a bull rider on a bull.

Trulane's body began to struggle under the weight of the GateKeeper, struggling for more air. The GateKeeper placed his gloved hands around Trulane's throat and squeezed as hard as it could; Trulane's body stiffened and convulsed several times before going completely still. A final release of air seemed to make a little hiss as it escaped from Trulane's dead lips. The GateKeeper inhaled this last breath into it's own mouth, and then screamed a final tortured howl of glee.

Forced to sit and watch the taking of his brother's soul, John was now on the verge of complete madness. The look in John's eyes revealed a complete loss of any connection to what he once thought of as reality. He watched as the ghastly figure dismounted Trulane's motionless body and stood at the side of the bed, it now turned it's ugly gaze to John. The GateKeeper pointed a finger in John's direction and shook it at him.

"Am I to be next?" John managed this muted thought to himself, as he sat helpless in that big leather chair.

The GateKeeper moved away from John and the bed, it was in the center of the room now. Once again the semi-solid form of the creature began to liquefy into a foul smelling mist, swirling around the room. The mist continued to rise until it met the ceiling of the room with a bright flash of light and then nothing but total blackness, and the creature was gone.

Everything went dark, nothing existed, and blackness filled the room. John lost his grip with consciousness and sat limp in the chair.

All was still, very still.

* CHAPTER NINE *

The snow that had been falling all night, finally stopped, but not before blanketing the village of Favisham with several inches of the white stuff. The early morning sun was just rising in the east, casting long shadows on the rows of small, thatched roof cottages, which lined the hillside surrounding Favisham Castle.

One house had a darker shadow then the others.

The good Doctor Raymond slowly entered the room; he gently closed the bedroom door behind him.

"I'm so sorry Mrs. Garwood, there was really nothing that could be done for your daughter, she has passed away," Doctor Raymond said as he tried to console the woman sitting by the window.

The woman's eyes had long since glazed over and swelled from too much sorrow and tears. She slowly lifted her head and paused for a moment before speaking to the Doctor.

"Yes, I know you did all that you could, it's just that Catherine was our only child, I don't know how we will go on with out her.

She pulled a white handkerchief from the pocket of her apron and wiped at her running nose. The old woman stood and slowly walked over to Doctor Raymond.

"I've sent word to my husband at Favisham Castle, Jarvis should be arriving soon," she said with a tear in her eye and a quiver in her voice.

"I don't know how we will go on without our beloved Catherine," she repeated.

"So many people have fallen ill this year, the sickness has sparred no one, why even at this very moment, your husband's employer; Trulane Wiseman is on his death bed at Castle Favisham." The doctor added.

"Yes, Jarvis told me of his illness and that his brother John had come to be at his side," said the sniffling woman.

"I have to make a call on him yet this morning, I'm afraid that he hasn't long to live. It would seem that this plague makes no difference in its choice of victims, rich or poor, they are all the same when it comes time to die."

Doctor Raymond began to gather up his medical instruments and place them carefully into his rolled, black leather bag. He retrieved a bottle of pills from the bag.

"Here, I want you to take two of these before you go to bed tonight, they should help you fall asleep," he said as placed the bottle on the table.

"Thank you Doctor," Mrs. Garwood sighed.

"I know that this is tough, but, when your husband gets home, have him bring Catherine's body down to my office at the morgue. I can start the embalming process when I get back from Favisham Castle. I shouldn't be long."

The Doctor looked up at the large ornate grandfather clock across the room, and noted the time. The beautifully carved wood clock seemed strangely out of place in this most modest of homes. There was a message printed on a brass plate affixed to the front of the clock, it read;

"PRESENTED TO JARVIS GARWOOD, IN RECOGNITION OF TWENTY FIVE YEARS OF FAITHFULL SERVICE. RICHARD L. WISEMAN."

"As I said, have Jarvis bring Catherine's body to my office. The one thing that might help bring you solace, is that Catherine will be buried in Favisham Cemetery. There are only two grave sites left and after those are filled the gates will be locked forever, after that any new burials will have to take place over in Port Town at the community cemetery and that is over seventy five miles drive from here. At least Catherine will be interred close to you," Dr. Raymond said, still trying to console the old woman.

"There now, please try and get some rest if you can, there is nothing more to be done."

The old woman approached the Doctor and took hold of his hand; she managed to thank him for all that he had done.

"Thank you good Sir," she said through a veil of tears.

The Doctor finished gathering his medical items and exited the little cottage. After securing everything in his carriage, Dr. Raymond climbed into the driver's seat and took hold of the reins, he cracked the leather strap against the backside of his single horse and he was off on his way.

The dirt roads were ice covered and frozen, making the ride to Favisham Castle slow and rough. A few minutes into his journey, Dr. Raymond took notice of another coach approaching from the other direction.

"This must be Jarvis Garwood, speeding home to meet with the pain of loosing his daughter," the doctor thought to himself.

The coach did not slow as it went thundering past Dr. Raymond, a man dressed in blue velvet, whipped at the team of horses, trying to coax as much speed from them as he could. Little does Jarvis Garwood know that he is already too late. His little girl is dead.

Doctor Raymond turned his attention back to the road in front of him and skillfully maneuvered his coach along the rutted trail.

"At this speed, it will most likely take the best part of an hour to get to the castle," Doctor Raymond spoke out-loud.

"I'll make a quick check on Mr. Wiseman and then head back to the office and finish up there with Catherine

Garwood, maybe then, I can finally get some well needed rest," he thought to himself.

* CHAPTER TEN *

Mr. Quince woke at the crack of dawn. Thin slivers of light, streamed through the bedroom window, bits of dust in the air were visible in the beams of sunlight as they danced around the room. Mr. Quince sat on the edge of his bed watching this ballet of light.

There was crispness to the air this morning; the last few embers glowed softly in the fireplace. Mr. Quince stretched one more time before finally getting out of his bed. He retrieved his slippers from under the bed and quickly slid them on to protect his feet from the cold floor. His dressing robe was on the garment stand at the foot of the bed where it had been neatly folded the night before. Mr. Quince shuffled his feet across the cold hardwood floor as he made his way over to the stack of dried wood next to the fireplace; he carefully selected two pieces of wood and gently placed them on top of the still glowing ember at the bottom of the fire box. He waited and watched until the new logs began to burn on their own. After washing his hands in the small basin of water that was in his room, Mr. Quince headed out into the hallway. He would peek in on Trulane and John, before heading down to the kitchen to start breakfast.

When Mr. Quince reached Trulane's bedroom, he put his hand on the brass door latch to open the door; it was ice cold to the touch. As the door swung open, a blast of bone chilling air seemed to rush out of the room and brush its bitter fingers across his face. He braced himself before continuing on.

Mr. Quince stepped through the doorway and into the room. The room was ice cold; the fire must have gone out many hours ago. The sight that lay before him was not what he had expected to find.

"Oh my God, my God, no!" he shouted as he ran to the bedside of his employer.

John Wiseman laid Slumped over the dead body of his brother, as if he too, might be dead.

Mr. Quince saw no movement from either brother.

"Master John, Master John, are you alright sir? Please Sir, please answer", Mr. Quince pleaded as he touched the shoulder of his master.

John began to moan as he was waking. He slowly raised himself up off of Trulane's body.

"Oh Sir, you gave me quite a scare, here, let me help you back to your chair," Mr. Quince was relieved to see that Master John was all right.

"Quince, Quince, my brother is dead," John grabbed at the collar of Mr. Quince's robe and repeated himself, "My brother is dead."

"Yes, yes I see that Sir, please sit back down in your chair and try and calm yourself."

"Calm myself? How can I calm myself when I have just witnessed such a terror filled night?" John questioned.

"Please Sir, there is nothing that can be done for Trulane, his suffering is over," Mr. Quince said, as he walked back over to the bed and pulled the sheet up over Trulane's head. He couldn't help noticing the peaceful expression on the dead man's face as he covered it.

"Look Master John, after months of pain and illness, and long tortured nights of fever, your brother is finally at rest," he said as he turned back to face John, who was now sitting in the chair.

The look of fear on John's face was in stark contrast to the peaceful smile on Trulane.

"I saw him come for my brother last night," John said.

"Who Sir? Whom did you see?" asked Mr. Quince.

"I saw the GateKeeper; he came in as a thief in the night."

"Tell me Master John, what exactly took place?"

"First it was just a fine mist with a nauseating smell, and then it took on form and some solidity." John tried to describe the horrible events of that night.

"Why did you not call me to come and help?" asked Mr. Quince.

"I was unable to move, as if two iron arms were wrapped around me, holding me fast to my chair. I tried screaming to you, but my voice too was paralyzed. I was totally trapped and unable to lift a finger to help my brother. I was forced to witness the whole thing."

John was getting himself all worked up again.

"How awful Sir," Mr. Quince could see the horror in John's eyes and his expression was that of someone on the verge of madness.

"Please try and calm yourself Sir," Mr. Quince repeated.

"The creature laughed at me as it literally sucked the life out of Trulane. It wanted me to suffer in agony; it enjoyed me watching as it took my brother's soul. I was trapped and not able to help. My pain and struggle seemed to only fuel the fierceness of the beast. At some point I must have blacked out, I don't remember anything more until you came in just now."

"Come Sir, we must get you out of this cold room and into some warm clothes. The Doctor is do to return this morning, he will help you with the necessary arrangements for the internment of your brother's body at Favisham Cemetery."

Mr. Quince helped John back to his own room, where he could get cleaned up and dressed. He made sure to build a roaring fire in John's fireplace before leaving the room. He would return to his own room at the other end of the castle so that he too could clean and change.

Mr. Quince was in the kitchen now; he was standing at the stove frying up some cornmeal mush for Master John's breakfast.

John came into the room and sat himself down at the rough wooden table in the center of the kitchen.

"I'll have your breakfast ready in one moment Sir," Mr. Quince assured his new master.

"How can I eat, with the knowledge that my brother's lifeless body is just upstairs?" John asked rhetorically.

"But eat you must Sir. You must be strong, so that you can stand up to the trying days ahead. There will be many details of your brother's affairs that will have to be put in order," said Mr. Quince.

"Yes, I realize that," John admitted as the plate of fried mush was set on the table before him. He took up his spoon and began to move the unappetizing food around on his plate. John finally gave in; he shoveled a few spoonfuls of the mush into his mouth, and swallowed hard.

The loud clanging sound of a huge iron bell tore through the silence of the morning, interrupting Mr. Quince, as he was just about to speak. It took a moment for the sound to make sense; it was the bell outside of the castle gate.

"My word, who could be ringing that bell? No one ever uses that bell, Jarvis is always on duty to greet and to give access to the castle grounds, where could he have run off to?" asked Mr. Quince.

Doctor Raymond stood outside the castle gate, rubbing his hands together, trying to rid off the bitter morning cold. He pulled on the knotted old rope once more and the bell gave out another loud clang.

"Surely, someone has heard that," the Doctor mumbled as he climbed back into his coach and wrapped a wool shawl around his shoulders. He would wait a few more minutes to see if someone comes to the gate.

Finally, a young boy who had been working in the stables heard the bell ringing and came walking down the road to the front gate.

A few minutes later, back in the castle's kitchen, the young stable boy comes bursting in, "Excuse me good sirs, but Doctor Raymond has arrived, he is in the main hall, I told him that you would be with him shortly."

"Very well boy," said John.

"Boy, hold on one moment, where is Jarvis this morning?" asked Mr. Quince.

"Sir, his daughter has died. She passed on earlier this morning. Mr. Jarvis left to be at his wife's side," he answered.

"Very well," Mr. Quince dismissed the lad from the kitchen.

"That is too bad about Jarvis's daughter and all, but I have my own family member to mourn," John remarked to Mr. Quince as he got up from the table.

"I will join you shortly, let me clear these dishes and then I will be up," offered Mr. Quince.

"No need, he was my brother and I will see to his remaining needs," John added as he exited the kitchen and went out into the main hall to escort Doctor Raymond up to Trulane's room.

"Come with me Doctor," John said without so much as a good morning.

John took the Doctor by the arm and the two men walked briskly up the flight of stairs and down the long hall, finally coming to a stop outside Trulane's closed bedroom door. John opened the door very slowly, not sure if he wanting to see the lifeless body of his brother again so soon. Only after a short pause, did John muster the nerve to enter.

Dr. Raymond pushed his way past John and walked to the bed and removed the sheet that covered Trulane's face.

"It's peaceful for him now, he no longer has to go through such agony and pain, even his expression is one of great calm," the Doctor said as he replaced the sheet.

"What will you do with Trulane's body now?" asked John, as he stood by the door, still fearful of reentering the room where he had witnessed his brother's death.

"Have one of your drivers bring a flatbed wagon and a team of horses around to the front of the house; they can follow me back to the morgue with your brother's body. I want to run a few tests on him before sending the body over to Brown's Mortuary for the embalming process."

John went back out into the hallway and summoned Mr. Quince; he relayed the doctor's request to his servant and went back to Trulane's doorway.

"They will be bringing the wagon around at once," he told the doctor.

"Good, now if you will come here and take hold of your brother's feet and legs, I will take his arms and shoulders and we can get him down stairs."

"I can not enter this cursed room, Mr. Quince will assist you," John said as he backed out of the doorway once more.

"The sooner I can get him to my office the better, I have Mr. Garwood's daughter to tend to first. There is one good thing however, your brother and Jarvis's little girl both have the honor of being the last two people buried in Favisham graveyard before it is closed for good," said the doctor.

That caught John's attention; there was no way in hell that his brother was going to be the last one buried in that cemetery. John forgot his fear of going into the room and rushed over to Dr. Raymond.

"You must make sure that my brother is buried before that servant's daughter, she can spend eternity guarding the graveyard, not my brother," John said as he grabbed the doctor's arm, jerking him off balance for a moment.

"Please, get a hold of yourself, what are you talking about?" the doctor asked as he pulled free from John's grip on his arm.

John went on to tell Dr. Raymond of his previous night's ordeal and the horrifying things that he had witnessed. The Doctor was not one to fall for such outlandish superstitions and fears; he assured John that this was just a figment of his over stressed mind.

"Why don't you let me give you something to calm you down, I know how difficult this must be," he said.

"Don't patronize me, I know what I saw, just do as I ask. My brother must not be the last one in that cemetery."

Mr. Quince arrived and assisted Dr. Raymond with Trulane's now stiff body. They carefully carried Trulane into the hall, down the steep staircase and out the front door to the waiting flatbed wagon. After making sure all was secure, the Doctor headed over to his own coach, John grabbed at Doctor Raymond's arm once again and pleaded his case.

"You must do as I have asked," he said.

"I will do what I can, but I believe that you are just being a bit unreasonable about this GateKeeper thing, now if you will please let go of my arm, I will be on my way."

"If you do not do as I have asked, you have no idea just how unreasonable I can be," John added.

Doctor Raymond shrugged and shook his head; "I will see what I can do."

John and Mr. Quince watched as the two carriages made their way down the cobblestone drive and out onto the main road.

John turned to Mr. Quince, "I will make sure that my brother is not the last one buried in Favisham Graveyard, you mark my words."

The two men returned to the warm confines of Favisham Castle.

* CHAPTER ELEVEN *

It is Friday, late afternoon; the snow is falling once again over the little village of Favisham; two days have past since Trulane's tragic death. His body lays in repose inside the sanctuary of the First Brethren Church of England.

The church is a huge structure made of dark stone that is weathered with age, there are two steeple towers and at the far end of the building a spire that reaches out and up into the sky. The church has stood in the town square for over three hundred years. Trulane's body is in the main sanctuary, while Catherine Garwood is in a smaller chapel set off to one side.

Outside, dozens of wagons and coaches, along with two finely decorated, black, horse drawn hearses line the avenue of the town square. The funeral coaches are equipped with viewing windows trimmed in brass; at each corner glows a small oil lamp. It takes a team of three horses to pull each hearse. Printed on the side of each hearse is the name, "BROWN'S FUNERARY," this was the only undertaker business in all of Favisham, it was a family business run by the father and son team of George the elder and Bruce K.

The undertakers had seen to all of the embalming needs of both Trulane and Catherine, they even offered to provide the mourners with alter music in the chapel, if desired. John had declined the offer of music, as it was just a waste of money to him, while the Garwood family chose to have the younger Brown play sacred songs on his lute.

Reverend Darwin Hunt has led the church for the last fifty years. A tall man of dark complexion, who is now well into his nineties and moves a lot slower in both walk and talk, but still has the respect of the villagers.

Visitors are still arriving for Trulane's funeral service. The Garwood funeral is already in progress. The good Reverend Hunt is busy delivering his service to a room full of grief stricken mourners. Mr. Jarvis Garwood, clad in his signature blue velvet pants and waistcoat, sits quietly next to his wife in the front row of chairs, their sorrow visible on both of their faces. Mrs. Garwood pulls a linen handkerchief from the pocket of her simple black peasant dress and wipes the tears from her eyes and cheek.

"My fellow towns men and ladies, it is a sad day in Favisham when the life of a young child is lost," the reverend was just finishing up his service.

"How does one justify a young life cut short by such a dreadful sickness," the reverend continued.

Meanwhile, John stands impatiently inside the mostly empty main chapel, at the side of his brother's casket; it's a smooth, dark oak wood coffin with brass fittings and trim. There is a fine silver inlay on the lid of the coffin that scrolls from one end up to a small plate that bares the name of the deceased; Trulane Wiseman. On either side of this plaque, are two finely carved angels inlaid with gold and silver. The casket is truly one fit for a man of nobility.

There are only a dozen or so people in the main chapel that have come to pay their respects to Trulane Wiseman. In attendance are a few town folk, the local constable, Mr. Cransten the family lawyer, Doctor Raymond and of course Mr. Quince. It would seem that the majority of visitors, in fact a majority of the whole town of Favisham was here to support the grief stricken Garwood family in their time of great loss. There had always been a separation of the poor working class and the wealthy land owners in Favisham. The plain hard working village people stayed with their own kind.

John pulls his precious jeweled watch from his vest and notes the time; he whirls the watch around by its chain a few times and returns it to his pocket. He makes a frustrated expression; John is obviously growing very impatient.

"It will be dark by the time we get out of here," John says as he walks over to Mr. Quince, "old Reverend Hunt is taking forever with that servant girl's service, perhaps you should go over there and have him hurry things up a bit. Trulane must not be the last one buried today, now go and..."

"I shall do no such thing Sir," Mr. Quince interrupted, "the Garwood family deserve to have this day unspoiled by you, Jarvis Garwood has served your family and brother for a very long time and I will not do as you ask of me. Trulane would not have you do such a thing as this, to the Garwood family," Mr. Quince said in a firm tone of voice.

This was the first time that Mr. Quince had ever disobeyed a direct order from a Wiseman. Mr. Quince could see the anger building inside the eyes of his employer. He began to walk away from John.

"How dare you refuse my order," John was furious with his servant.

"Who needs you anyway, I'll do it myself," John spouted as he pushed his way past Mr. Quince and started toward the small chapel.

"Ashes to ashes, dust to dust...," said Reverend Hunt.

As John approached the small chapel, he could hear that the service was just concluding, he grunted something to himself and decided to return to the almost empty main sanctuary and his brother's body.

Mr. Quince was now standing on the other side of the room; he was obviously trying to keep as much distance as possible between he and John Wiseman.

John could hear that the service for Catherine Garwood was finally drawing to an end. People began to move out of the little chapel, offering their respects to Mr. and Mrs. Garwood as they filed out and into the cold.

"Such a tragedy, such a waste, if we can be of any help in this time of need, please don't hesitate to ask," offered one older woman.

"Thank you so much," replied Mrs. Garwood as she continued to wipe away tears.

Once all of the family members and mourners had cleared the little chapel, it was time to move the small coffin. With the help of a few townsmen, the two undertakers, George and Bruce, carried Catherine's simple casket out the chapel doors and down the front steps to the waiting horse drawn hearse.

John was growing increasingly impatient, "how much longer must this take?" he yelled, not caring who might hear, "my brother must not be left behind and made to suffer all eternity."

"Yes, yes, please calm yourself good Sir," Reverend Hunt said as he passed by John, "please if you will be seated, we will begin with the benediction for the dead."

John sat down all by himself in the pew closest to Trulane's coffin; he sat nervously on the edge of the seat, wishing that this would be over as soon as possible.

John raised his hand and made a whirling motion at the Reverend, "then please, let's get this over with," he demanded.

Meanwhile, outside the church, George the elder Brown and the hearse containing the body of Catherine Garwood, slowly pulls away, followed by a long line of coaches on their way to the cemetery. The procession moves at a slow and dignified manner, to show respect for the dead and for the grieving.

* CHAPTER TWELVE *

Inside the main sanctuary of the church, John sits uncomfortably in his seat; he checks the time on his precious pocket watch, noting that the day is growing late, he shifts from side to side on the hard wooden pew. John is aware that the sun has already begun to set and that the Garwood funeral procession is already on its way to the graveyard, if he intends to get Trulane buried first, he must end this delay right now.

The good Reverend Hunt had been slowly delivering his service, taking too much time as far as John was concerned. He had finally had enough; John jumped up from his seat.

"You must hurry this up," John prompted the preacher.

"The Garwood funeral procession is already on its way to the cemetery, perhaps we can finish this service at the graveyard," John asserted.

"Mr. Wiseman, the Garwood funeral has nothing to do with your brother, so please be so kind as to sit back down and I will get through this as quick as possible, please Mr. Wiseman," Reverend Hunt replied.

"How dare you presume to tell me what to do," John shouted back at the preacher.

"Please Sir, let us show a little respect for the dead," the preacher pleaded to John to show a bit more compassion.

John walked up to the front of the sanctuary; he raised his hand and pointed a finger directly at the old preacher.

"If I say that we are going to finish this service at the graveyard, then that is precisely what you will do," he demanded.

"I do not know what this is all about and I will not take part in such an insult to your brother's good memory. You can either, be seated and let me continue or, have it your way and bury your brother without a proper holy service. The choice is yours," said Reverend Hunt.

John did not return to his seat, he turned to the few mourners that sat quietly in their pews and began to address them directly.

"Everyone in this room knows the legend of the GateKeeper. I tell you, the legend is real," he began.

"I witnessed the ghastly thing with my own eyes the night that my brother died. You have all heard the stories since you were little; the spirit of the last person buried in a cemetery is doomed to guard the bodies of those that went before him. That soul is destined to remain in torment for all eternity as the GateKeeper. The last one to be buried today at Favisham Cemetery will be the GateKeeper forever."

John waited to see if there was any reaction from those in the room. Not one person spoke.

"Mr. Wiseman if this is the case, then it is all that more important that Trulane receive his proper holy burial," added the Reverend.

John did not want to listen to the preacher.

"If any of you have ever been friends of my family, then please help me now. I must get my brother's body to the cemetery," John was pleading with anyone and everyone in the room.

Not getting any support from those in the room, John decided to take matters into his own hands.

"Very well, if none of you will help me, I'll do it myself," John declared.

He walked up to the front of the chapel where Trulane's coffin sat resting on top of a wheeled table. He looked at Trulane's body one more time before closing the lid of the casket. The visions of the GateKeeper and his mocking death grin were still so vivid in John's mind.

"Here, here, you can't do that," demanded Reverend Hunt.

"You are disrespecting the memory of your good brother."

"It would be more disrespectful if I were to let him be doomed to the fate of the Gatekeeper," John replied.

John started to wheel the table and casket of his dead brother down the aisle toward the exit.

"I can not let you do this," the reverend said as he put a hand on the casket, "you must stop this lunacy."

John grabs the reverends hand in his and rips it free from the casket. He pushes on by the preacher and continues down the aisle.

Mr. Brown's son Bruce, who had been standing at the chapel exit, finally offers to help with the coffin of Trulane Wiseman.

The sun had long since gone down and a severe snowstorm had begun to blanket the whole village. John and his helper managed to get Trulane's coffin loaded into the back of the waiting hearse.

"I'll be riding up there with you," John informed Bruce.

John vaulted to the top of the carriage and sat next to the black hooded driver.

"Let's go driver, take hill road to the cemetery," John instructed.

"But Sir, the hill route will be too dangerous!" objected the driver.

"There will be more traffic and people on that road Sir, and it's very slippery this time of year to try and navigate the hills," the driver continued.

"Do what you are being paid for and mind your mouth, you fool," John was growing impatient.

"You will follow my directions and drive this hearse where I tell you. We must be the first to reach the cemetery; if we take hill road we can beat the Garwood family. Now do as you are told."

Bruce swallowed back his pride and took hold of the horse's reins. He turned the team of horses toward Hill road. With a flick of his whip on the backside of his lead horse the carriage pulled away from the church. The wheels of the hearse struggled to get a grip in the fresh fallen snow causing the rig to slide to one side of the road and then to the other.

"Faster, we must go faster," John shouted.

"Sir, it is much too slippery to travel any faster," Bruce said as he tried to maintain his grip on the reins.

"If we are too late to bury my brother before that common Garwood girl, I will personally hold you responsible and will do everything in my power to ruin both you and your father," John threatened.

"The fate of my brother and that of you and your father's business is in your hands. If my brother is doomed for eternity, I put that responsibility firmly in your lap and will hold you and your family accountable. Is that what you want?" John asked of his driver.

"No Sir, I don't want that at all," Bruce answered.

"Then do as you are told," John said in a firm voice as he pulled his watch out one more time. "We can beat the Garwoods, now hurry, hurry, we must get there first."

The driver braced against his seat, he took a firm hold of the reins in one hand and raised his whip high over head with the other hand. He whirled the whip twice in the air and brought it forward with a loud crack that split the air.

"Ha, ha, come on," the driver coaxed his team of horses to run faster.

He cracked the whip once more and snapped it across the backside of the horses.

The team of horses reacted. First they reared up a little, pawing at the air with their front hooves and then lunged forward with all of the might that they could muster. They dug there feet into the snow and pulled with everything that they had. The coach slid from side to side on the road as the horses poured out more and more strength, their bodies tensed against the hearse's heavy load.

"That's it, faster, faster," John was shouting as the coach continued to gain speed, "Faster, faster," he continued to yell.

Bruce cracked the whip one more time.

The heavy, coffin bearing coach managed to get a good running start on the snow covered trail, they would need that speed to make it up the steep incline of Hill Road.

Again and again the driver cracked his whip and the hearse would fish tail from side to side as it picked up more and more speed.

"Yes, that's it. If we can muster the speed we need to get to the top of Hill Road, we shall surely beat the others to Favisham Cemetery," John continued to shout encouragement at the driver sitting right next to him.

And so, under a dark snow filled sky, the race was truly on, a race against time eternal.

* LUCKY THIRTEEN *

The Garwood Funeral procession continued on it's slow dignified pace through the main streets of Favisham. The hearse was in front, driven by the elder Brown, followed by a small coach containing Mr. and Mrs. Garwood, behind that, stretched a long line of coaches and wagons winding their way through town. Oil lamps that glowed against the snow, lighted the village streets. Small shops displayed their goods in windows along the village roads. Most of the owners had closed their stores and were lending their support to the Garwood family in their time of grief.

The Garwood funeral had made good, steady time and was now within sight of the cemetery gates.

John sat firmly on top of the hearse next to the young undertaker, his hands gripped hard at the seat rail as the driver continued to push his team of horses to the top of the hill.

"Out of the way, you fool!" John yelled, as a well dressed, man just seemed to pop out of nowhere and into their path.

Seeing the hearse just in time, the man jumps back to the side of the road, and seeks safety behind a large tree.

"Hey, you almost ran me down," the man blurted as he shook his fist in the air.

John leaned over to his driver, "That old fool should be glad that we didn't grind his body into the cobblestones," laughing as he spoke.

Bruce paid no mind to John's comment; he was too intent on watching the road.

The hearse swerved around the last bend in the trail before the top of the hill, and slid wildly to one side as the driver fought to bring the rig under control. He brought the hearse to an abrupt stop at the top of Hill Road. The horses snorted with exhaustion as they stomped their feet.

John leaned over the side of the coach and peered inside one of the glass viewing windows of the hearse. He could see that Trulane's casket was still securely in its place.

"Why are you stopping?" John asked as he turned back to his driver.

"Sir, we can not continue at such a dangerous pace, we will surely have an accident, the road is not safe," was the drivers reply.

John tried to look down the hill to see if he could catch any sight of the Garwood hearse, straining to see through the now heavy blowing snow, he could just make out the faint glow of the oil lamps that hung on the side of the hearse bearing Catherine Garwood's body.

"Nonsense, we are almost there, the Garwoods haven't buried their dead daughter yet, we can still beat them and get my brother in the ground first, we've just a little further to go, now do what you were hired for," John shouted back at the driver.

The driver did not want to argue. He turned his attention back to his team of horses and gave the command for them to resume their task of delivering the body of Trulane Wiseman to his final resting-place.

The coach stormed down the narrow winding road.

"Faster, faster. Keep those horses moving, we must be first, we must," John continued his shouting.

"I can not run the horses this fast down a hill Sir, I must slow down or we will surely have an accident," warned the driver.

"Keep going you fool," John yelled.

"I demand that you do as you are told."

Disregarding John's demand, Bruce began to pull back on the reins, trying to slow the coach down a bit.

"Damn you! Fool! Move, move over."

John tried pushing the driver to the side, fighting him for control of the coach. Bruce pushed back, but John was a much bigger man than he was. John took his elbow and jammed it as hard as he could into the driver's right side. The driver doubled over in his seat. He struggled to keep control of the now out of control hearse as it stormed down the road. The horses continued to pull with all of their might.

John Wiseman had lost all control of his actions; he pulled back a clinched fist and sent a solid blow across the driver's head. Bruce was knocked off balance; John seized the chance and pushed his driver from the coach. Bruce rolled several times head over heels in the snow, he smashed heavily into a pile of large boulders, striking his head and finally ending up sprawled out by an old oak tree at the side of the road, and he lay motionless.

John held the reins tight as he took control of the coach.

"Go now you beasts, faster," he tried to coax more speed.

The hearse raced by the last few houses in this part of Favisham. The town cemetery was just around the corner and John was sure that he could still beat the Garwood family in this race to the grave. But, as John got closer to the graveyard gates, he could see that alas, he might be too late to save his brother's soul after all.

There they stood, all the village people, gathered around Catherine Garwood's coffin as it was being carried from its hearse to the gravesite.

John knew that this would be his only hope, he must hurry. The race was not yet over by any means. Catherine Garwood's body was not in the ground; John still had the slimmest of chances. He aimed the speeding coach at the graveyard gates.

* CHAPTER FOURTEEN *

Catherine Garwood's coffin was placed on top of three wooden braces that stretched across the open hole in the ground that would become her final grave. A series of ropes and pulleys were connected to the handles of her casket. These ropes would then be used to slowly lower the coffin into the hole. Two, dirt covered old men stood off to one side, leaning on their shovels; one was a short stout fellow with a bald head, he was wrapped in layers of heavy clothes to fight off the blowing cold but yet he left his head bare. A half smoked cigar was clenched in the corner of his mouth, the curls of white smoke from the cigar mixed with the descending snow, swirled about his bald head. The taller of the two men, was of a thin build, he dressed much more lightly against the cold. He wore just a simple black wool coat with a scarf tied around his neck. It had been their job to dig the last two gravesites in Favisham cemetery. It would also be their job to fill in the two holes when everyone has left. For now, they just stood back and waited until they were needed.

It was well into the dark of night as the snow continued to fall in a heavy sheet of white. John drove the hearse directly through the graveyard gates and came to a sliding stop. The coach halted next to a big pile of dirt by the side of the small winding road. He looked around and determined that this was to be Trulane's grave.

It was true that the cemetery was filled to capacity; the hole that would be Trulane's last resting place looked as if it had been squeezed in between the road and the edge of the front gate of the graveyard. This fact would have upset John at any other time, but for now all that mattered is that Trulane's body be laid to rest.

John strained his eyes in the night; he could just make out the glow of lanterns in the distance and the outline of mourners standing around a casket that was still held above its final abyss.

John knew that he must act quickly if he intended to beat that Garwood girl. He jumped down from his seat and lost his footing as he landed on the ground. John got back to his feet and ran around to the back of the hearse to check on his brother's casket. The horses were very spooked by all of this and would not stand still. They continually pulled at their bridles and bits. John had no other choice then to cut them loose from the coach and let them run. He pulled at several of the leather ropes that secured the horses to there leads, John managed to set them loose and all three ran off into the white dark night of what was now becoming a full fledged snow storm of giant proportions.

John turned his attention back to the task of unloading the casket. He removed one of the oil lamps from the side of the coach and set it down along side of the grave. John figured that he could handle this all by himself.

Now standing at the back of the hearse, John realized that the heavy glass doors were secured shut by a large brass lock. Not having possession of the key, John looked around on the ground and found the next best thing, a rock. He raised the piece of stone up over his right shoulder and brought it forward smashing the engraved glass.

"Ouch, damn," John shouted as he felt the sharp edge of a piece of glass cut deep into his hand.

Blood filled the palm of his hand in an instant. He reached into his pocket and pulled out a fine gentleman's handkerchief. John winced from the pain as he wrapped the cloth around his hand to try and stop the flow of blood; he tied it as tight as he could.

Using his other hand John managed to open the back doors of the hearse; he positioned himself at the foot of the casket and began to pull.

"Come on, come on," John talked out loud as he struggled with the weight of the coffin.

"Damn, don't do this to me," he needed better leverage.

John stopped his pulling and got up inside the back of the hearse, he managed to crawl over the coffin and get to the head of Trulane's casket. Now he could use all of his strength to push the casket out of the coach. John braced himself and gave one hard push; the casket broke free and slid out the end of the hearse, crashing to the snow covered ground.

John jumped down from the coach and grabbed hold of one of the casket handles, he began to drag Trulane's coffin through the snow like it was some sort of bizarre looking sled.

"Come on brother, we can do this," he was now mumbling out loud, talking to his dead brother for support.

"Just a little further now, it won't be much longer dear brother," John continued.

John paused at the edge of the grave pit that opened its black mouth up to him. He looked around and could see that the Garwood funeral was just finishing, they would begin to lower her casket down into the grave now.

John pulled his prize jeweled pocket watch out of his vest pocket and held it close to the oil lamp; he noted the time and threw the precious watch to the dirt, no longer caring for the value of the thing. He turned back to his brother's coffin, John slid his way down to the bottom of the grave, it was so dark down there in that hole, and with the snow blowing and John could not even see the faint glow of his own oil lamp. John reached up using both hands now and found a hold on one of the casket handles, he braced himself as best as he could and with one great pull the casket fell forward into the hole. The coffin had nearly pinned John into the grave as well. Freeing himself, he scrambled his way up out of the grave and ran back to the hearse and retrieved the shovel that was strapped to its frame.

Not wasting any time, John climbed to the top of the dirt pile at the edge of the grave. He began to shovel franticly. First one then two then three shovel loads of dirt landed on top of Trulane's casket.

John was breathing heavy now as he continued to throw dirt over the top of the coffin. The blood from his cut had saturated through the handkerchief and a fresh flow of red was now running down John's hand and dripping onto the dirt that was being thrown into the hole.

After a thin layer of dirt covered the lid of the casket, John was satisfied that his brother was in the ground and buried before the Garwood girl. He had kept his promise toTrulane.

"We did it," John shouted as he threw the shovel down to the ground.

John picked up his lantern and held it high in the air so that he could try and get a better look at his surroundings. He was stunned to realize that Trulane's grave was actually very close to the place where their father had been laid to rest. John made his way a little closer to his father's engraved tombstone. He held the oil lamp up so that he could read the name on the stone.

"My father, I can still remember the grand funeral that the town had for you," he was talking out loud.

He thought to himself how the Wiseman name had really stood for something back then. Now, it will be the laughingstock of the village. Those that believe in the old superstition of the Gatekeeper will feel my pain, while those towns' folk that do not believe will surely call me mad.

"I did see the Gatekeeper. I am not mad," John shouted into the night.

His eyes blazed wide and wild as he began to scream louder and louder, "I am not mad, I'm not I tell you," he continued to repeat himself over and over.

John tried to negotiate his way back to Trulane's grave but he stumbled and dropped his lamp sending it crashing to the snow covered ground. John regained his footing as best as he could and stood at the edge of the partially filled hole. He began to dance around the grave like some madman. His arms flailing in the air over his head.

"Hee Hee, we did it, we did it, we cheated the Gatekeeper, the Gatekeeper," John was singing as he danced. He was screaming and running around his brother's grave, he had truly lost all sense of reality. John ran off into the darkness of the cemetery, slamming into one head stone after another, lost in his own insanity.

* CHAPTER FIFTEEN*

"And so now we do commit the body of Catherine Garwood to the safety of her final peaceful rest, Ah man," Reverend Hunt finished with his grave side prayer.

"So in closing this service, I would like you all to bow your head in a moment of silence for this poor girl and her family."

The many towns' people quietly bowed their heads. After a few moments of prayer, the villagers all went to pay their final respects to Mr. and Mrs. Garwood one last time.

One by one they all began to return to the safety of their coaches, away from the blowing cold. The mortician, George Brown, escorted the overly distraught Mrs. Garwood to his awaiting hearse and drove off into the darkness of the night. Mr. Jarvis Garwood was no where to be found. Perhaps he had some unfinished business to attend to. It would seem that all of the mourners had finally left the cemetery.

The two grounds keepers that had been leaning idly on their shovels earlier were now busy rigging the ropes and pulleys to Catherine's coffin in preparation of lowering the heavy box down into the grave. One of the men held onto the long length of rope that kept the casket dangling in mid air as the other man tried to center the load over the six foot hole.

"That's it, right there," one man yelled to the other, "go ahead, that's got it."

Carefully they lowered Catherine's coffin into the grave until it gently came to rest at the bottom. The two workers scrambled down into the grave and disconnected the ropes. They retrieved the shovels from near by and began shoveling spade load after spade load of dirt into Catherine's grave.

"Damn Thomas, let's hurry and get this done, it's freezing out here tonight," the taller of the two said to the other.

"It's not the cold Bartholomew, that's not what's getting to me, I just don't like being out here, something doesn't feel right, I can sense these things you know," Thomas replied to his boss.

"I know just what you mean. I've worked in this cemetery for over thirty years now and I can tell you that I've heard and seen many a strange thing in this old grave yard. Right now all of the hair on the back of my neck is standing on end. There is something strange at work tonight in this cemetery. Let's hurry and get finished with this so that we can get out of here," said Bartholomew.

It didn't take long for the two men to finish their work.

"Gather up those oil lamps and shovels and let's be on our way," Bartholomew said as he stamped his feet on the fresh dirt of Catherine's grave.

Thomas extinguished all but one of the lamps that had been set up around the grave. He managed to carry this last lamp along with the two shovels over to the coach where he and Bartholomew quickly loaded everything into the storage compartment at the back of the wagon; he managed to cram all of their tools into the small space.

"Ok, let's go Sir," Thomas said as he climbed into the coach along side of his boss.

The snow and wind continued to blow as the two of them headed out the cemetery gates, in fact it was blowing so hard that they did not notice the Wiseman hearse still parked near the front of the graveyard.

* CHAPTER SIXTEEN *

"At what point does a man's obsession turn to insanity? What degree of madness can one man take?" John thought to himself.

The blowing snow ripped at the skin of John's face as he sat huddled in the doorway of an old cemetery mausoleum. He had managed to find this little bit of shelter from the storm.

Ever so slowly, John began to regain some since of where he was.

"How long have I been here in this graveyard?" he wondered.

John raised his hands to his mouth and cupped them together. He blew into his frozen hands hoping to warm them with his breath. Once a little feeling had begun to return, John reached under his coat with his right hand; his fingers instinctively went to his vest pocket and began to feel around for his jeweled pocket watch. He fumbled around in his pocket for the watch. It was not there. John searched his other pockets but found nothing. He was confused and lost he had no memory of losing the watch. In fact, John could not remember how he had ended up hiding in this strange mausoleum.

John stood and leaned against the stone structure that had protected him. He squinted his eyes against the dark and blowing snow. John tried to get a glimpse of anything familiar that was around him, so that he might find his way back to Trulane's grave and to the exit of this hellish place.

The snow was blinding, it blotted out the blackness of the night. A lantern would be of little use, even if John had one.

So with a careful step, John left the semi safety of the mausoleum doorway.

Feeling his way from one tombstone to the next, he pulled himself along through the snow. The deep cut in John's hand had finally stopped bleeding; There was no feeling left at all in his hands. John looked down at his frozen hands and could see that they were turning a dark shade of blue, almost black in color. Frostbite had set in and the numbing pain was all that he could bare.

There was no way for John to even know what direction he was heading, but he continued to inch his way along. He would take three or four steps and then slip on the uneven frozen ground. More then once he found himself face down on the ground crawling on his hands and knees.

"I must get to Trulane's grave, then I can find my way out of this dreadful cemetery," John tried to build his confidence and not give up.

Every part of his body was burning from exposure to the extreme cold. Small Ice cycles had formed on his face and brow.

"It can't be much further," John thought, "I'm sure that the grave should be in this direction. If I can just find it, then I can get to the safety of the hearse and get out of here." John failed to remember that he had let the team of horses run loose from the hearse. Still, the coach would at least provide John with the protection and shelter that he needed.

John looses his footing one more time and again falls forward only this time his fall is broken by a marble grave stone smashing against the side of his head. John is on his knees, instantly a stream of warm blood begins to flow profusely from the slash in John's scalp. He raises his already bandaged hand to the wound but the numbness in his fingers prevents him from having any luck finding the cut in his scalp. He holds the palm of his hand to his head until the throbbing stops.

A few moments pass as John rests; he tries to shake off his dizziness and blurred vision.

"It can't be much further," John mutters as he pulls himself to his feet once more.

The wind and blowing snow has finally begun to ease up a bit, enough so that John can at least watch his footing a little closer. It is still black as coal in the cemetery; John soon begins to recognize the surrounding grave markers and realizes that Trulane's grave should be directly ahead of him.

"Right over here, it should be right over here," John inches his way forward until he is standing at the very edge of Trulane's grave.

"I'm here dear brother, I did not forsake you. I have kept my promises. May you rest in peace."

John looks around for the shovel that he had previously thrown to the ground in his earlier jubilant state of celebration. He starts to shovel dirt into Trulane's grave once again. The going is much tougher now, as the freezing air and snow has hardened the once soft dirt. It has been a long time since John has had to perform such hard physical labor. One spade full at a time the dirt landed in the hole, hardly making a difference.

Twenty minutes go by and John is still at it. His pace has slowed markedly do to the exhaustion that this night has brought. He pauses to catch his breath and get some relief from the pain that has begun to gnaw at the base of his back. He sets the shovel aside for a few moments and stands at the edge of the grave, looking deep into the blackness of its interior.

John lowers himself down on to his knees. He pauses for a moment of silence at the very edge of the grave.

He finally speaks;

"What will be my fate dear brother? Who will see to my burial when the time comes? Who will keep me safe from the Gatekeeper? I have no one dear brother. What will become of me?" John asks of his dead brother, "I have nobody!"

* CHAPTER SEVENTEEN *

A cold wind rushed through Favisham Cemetery, causing the snow to swirl up into the air forming white funnels across the landscape. More snow was falling now as John Wiseman knelt at the open grave. He had grown silent and motionless in the cold. John's eyes seemed to be frozen in a stare. He just kept gazing down into Trulane's grave, totally unaware of his surroundings.

"Thud, slash."

A sound suddenly caught John's attention. He raised his head up from its frozen stare and waited.

There it was again. The sound was coming from somewhere close at hand, but John could not tell from what direction.

"What is that sound?" John thought.

"Thud, slash, thud, slash," it was getting closer.

Then the sound suddenly stopped.

The wind and snow came to an abrupt stop.

Everything stopped; it was dead silent in the graveyard.

John felt his heart begin to pound in his chest; he could hear it beating in his ears. There was something evil about the feeling that was taking hold of John. He sensed that he was no longer alone. It was fear that held John in his place, he was afraid to move from his kneeling position.

Finally after what seemed like an eternity of silence, John managed to speak three simple words, "Please save me," he mumbled.

As the last syllable was uttered, John was struck in the small of his back by some heavy object. The force of the blow sent him flying forward off of his kneeling position. John tumbled face down into Trulane's grave, smashing through the lid of the coffin. He tried to raise himself from the splintered wood by shifting his weight but that only caused him to fall further into the coffin. John found that he was face to face with his dead brother.

"Awhhhhhhhh," John let out a scream.

He tried to pull free but somehow John had become tangled up on Trulane's body. He was stuck on something. John was unable to see up out of the six foot grave.

He was unable to see the gloved hand that was clutching the shovel, the shovel that came crashing down onto the back of John's head with a sickening sound.

Everything went black.

John was unconscious for a few short minutes. When he came around again and was aware of his surroundings he opened his eyes. Blood was spattered all over the white snow in front of him, it was his blood.

"Had the Gatekeeper come back for him? Would this be his time to die?" John wondered.

John listened for any sound. There was nothing.

John worked his way free and tried to get to his feet. He had to stand on his brother's body so that he might be able to reach the top.

"Forgive me, my brother," he said as he stood on Trulane's embalmed chest.

John scraped his once manicured fingernails into the dirt, digging his blood covered fingers into the wall of the grave. Climbing ever so slowly from the pit, John reaches up trying to find a good final grip.

His hands are cut and bleeding and numb from the cold, John manages to get a firm grip on something, something solid.

"Perhaps a tree root or something," John thought to himself.

He braced one foot against the side of Trulane's coffin and pulled with all of the strength that he had left to summon.

Up, up, an inch at a time, as long as his grip held, John was sure that he could free himself from this pit.

Approaching the top edge of the grave, John clawed along.

There was someone else standing at the edge of the grave, waiting, waiting for John.

A large black boot struck John in the face as he reached the top. The force of the kick split John's chin open and sent him tumbling back down into the freshly dug grave. After quickly shaking off this last blow, John tries to focus. He sees a light.

A lantern is lit and placed at the mouth of Trulane's grave. The light casts an eerie glow of blue onto the blood covered snow.

Looking up, John begins to recognize the shape standing above the grave, its features taking on those of a man.

Not just any man, but a man that John knew.

"You," John yelled.

"Why are you doing this? What do you want from me?" John was pleading for an answer.

Blood continued to pour from John's sliced chin. He wiped his frozen fingers across his eyes.

"What is it? Why?" John managed to ask.

The figure at the top of the grave remained silent, its two long arms slowly raising some object high above. The silhouette of the object now becomes clear, but John makes this realization a bit too late.

John's assailant hoists the blade of the shovel higher above its hooded head and pauses.

John has only one thought on his mind as the blade of the shovel comes crashing down into his head, splitting a wide gapping hole in to it, "Why?"

"Arggggggg, scccrumle, blup," John makes a hideous gurgling sound as he falls into a heap.

Consciousness is fading fast for John; he starts to sink into blackness.

A final blow from the blood covered shovel's blade separates John's neck at the base. He lays in a dead bloody heap along side his brother Trulane.

The figure standing above the grave throws the shovel to the side. He notices something glinting in the snow by his foot.

A gloved hand reaches into the blood splattered snow and retrieves a beautiful gold watch, one covered in jewels, one that once belonged to his victim.

He pushes the release catch on the watch and the cover swings open. He holds the watch up and takes note of the time. After a moment or two the gloved hand closes the watch and slowly tucks it safely away, away in its vest pocket, it's blue velvet vest.

Jarvis Garwood bends down and picks up the discarded shovel. He begins to throw one load of dirt into the grave and then another and another.

"My good daughter will not be the last one buried in this cemetery," Jarvis proclaims aloud.

"She will not be doomed to the fate of THE GATEKEEPER; I leave that to you John Wiseman. This is your fate; you will roam this old graveyard for eternity.

Jarvis finishes his gruesome work; as the first rays of the morning sunrise peek over the cemetery walls, at last the grave is filled in. Jarvis admires his work.

He must hurry, he must not be late, and he has to leave now if he wants to make it on time. Jarvis has never missed a day of work as THE GATEKEEPER OF FAVISHAM CASTLE.

THE END
BOOK TWO

At least until next time, that is. I hope you enjoyed my little tale.

Sweet Dreams.

P. T. LeeZard

Ω

ABOUT THE AUTHOR

The Gatekeeper is Mr. Buck's second book in the series of Cheap Chills thrillers. An avid traveler to the Caribbean, he enjoys exploring and snorkeling. He is a Philosopher and an amateur Magician, who lives with his wife, three cats an Irish setter and a bird in northern Indiana.